A Castle on Viola Street

DyAnne DiSalvo

HarperCollins*Publishers*

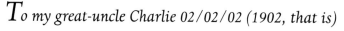

To my great-uncle Charlie 02/02/02 (1902, that is)

"All deuces, baby."

The author would like to acknowledge the following for their help with her book:
William Menke, Habitat for Humanity International
Doug Wagner, Metro Camden Habitat, New Jersey
The "Monday crew" at Sacred Heart of Camden, New Jersey

The art is done in gouache, colored pencil, and china marker.

A Castle on Viola Street

Library of Congress Cataloging-in-Publication Data
DiSalvo, DyAnne.
A castle on Viola Street / by DyAnne DiSalvo.
p.   cm.
Summary: A hardworking family gets their own house at last by joining a community
program that restores old houses.
ISBN 0-688-17690-9 — 0-688-17691-7 (lib. bdg.)
[1. Dwellings—Fiction.]   I. Title.
PZ7.D6224 Cas   2001   00-40889
[E]—dc21   CIP
AC

Typography by Stephanie Bart-Horvath
1 2 3 4 5 6 7 8 9 10
❖
First Edition

ABOUT HOUSING ORGANIZATIONS

While helping to build a house, a young woman said to me, "My family has a home; we just need a house to put it in!" Not long after that, a group of volunteers got together and helped her family build a simple, decent house where they could put their home.

About one billion people in the world today don't have a safe or affordable place to live. Some have lost their homes to natural disasters. Many live on small fixed incomes or may not make enough money to afford to rent or buy a house. Many people, including those in religious organizations, governments, corporations, and nonprofit organizations, are working hard to make this better.

In more than two thousand communities around the world, people who feel strongly about the need for housing have formed Habitat for Humanity affiliates. Affiliates are groups that bring together volunteers and resources to build simple houses. Habitat for Humanity homeowners pay for their houses in part with three hundred to five hundred hours of what is called "sweat equity." This means they must help build other people's houses as well as their own and also do other work with the affiliate.

Habitat for Humanity International, Christmas in April, World Vision, and the Local Initiatives Support Corporation are just a few of the organizations working to build houses and help communities develop the resources they need for success.

—Millard Fuller
Founder and President,
Habitat for Humanity International
Americus, Georgia

In the old days, before I was ten, we rented an apartment on Emerald Street. It was a small place to live in for one whole family, but somehow we made the room.

There always seemed to be enough to go around, even with five people at our table.

Every morning my father would get up even before the sun. "Someday things will change around here," he would whisper to me. He usually said this during the winter when the house was beginning to feel chilly. Then he'd kiss us good-bye, tuck up our blankets, and leave for his job at the diner.

My mother worked part-time in the downtown bakery while my sisters and I were at school. After school she'd sit on the stoop and watch us play.

Sometimes my mother would flip through a magazine. She'd show me pictures of houses with gardens and porches. They all looked like castles to me. I'd puff out my cheeks when I looked at our place. It was old and peeling and sorry.

That's when my mother would hug me and say, "Our family is rich in more ways than we can count."

On Saturday mornings my mother would weigh my pockets down with quarters for the Laundromat.

"Hold Andy's hand," she'd tell my sister.

Then my mother would slip two brown-bagged lunches in the wagon with a dollar for a treat. My sister and I would bump our cart to the Soap & Go on Viola Street.

Now, across the street from the Soap & Go were three boarded-up houses. My father said it was a shame. "Somebody should do something about that," he'd say whenever he saw them. So when a truck pulled up and workers unloaded equipment, I started to pay attention.

"What's going on over there?" a lady at the Soap & Go asked.

Mr. Rivera pointed to a flier that was posted up front.

"I'll bet it has something to do with this," he told her. The flier had a picture of a house and said YOU TOO CAN OWN A HOME.

After our laundry was dried and folded, I took my sister by the hand and rushed our wagon back to Emerald Street.

At supper I told my parents all about what I had heard and seen. My father scrambled eggs with extra zest, and my mother put ice in our water.

"There's a meeting tonight," I said. "Seven o'clock at the school."

Later on, when my parents came home, they were just as excited as I was.

"This organization buys empty houses and fixes them up like new!" said my mother.

"And if you're interested in helping to fix up a house for other people," my father continued, "then one day other people will help fix up a house for you."

That sounded like a good plan to me. It would be nice to live in a house that wasn't so chilly in winter.

"So we signed up," my father told me. "Can we count on you to help?"

I hugged them so tight I almost fell out of bed. I think they knew my answer.

Well, you know how sometimes, when you never believe that anything will ever be different, then one morning you just wake up and nothing is the same? That's what happened to our family that spring when the project on Viola Street began.

Clang! Bang! Bang! Smash! Those workers started early.

"Take a good look," my mother told us. "That's what we'll be doing soon."

"Are all those people getting a house?" I asked.

"Some of them will," my mother said. "But anyone who wants to can help. It's called volunteering."

Piece by piece, the inside of the first house came apart—one old bathtub, some cabinets, sinks. Slats of wood and piping piled up like a mountain full of junk in the Dumpster.

Most people on the block were happy about the project, but other people were not. The lady next door said, "No banging before nine o'clock!" Some people laughed and said out loud, "Who would want a house in a neighborhood like this?"

But my father would smile and whisper to me, "Sometimes new things are hard to get used to and people are slow to change."

On the weekends, when our family showed up, a leader called out the assignments.

"Everyone here will have a special job to do," she said.

My mother scraped wallpaper off crusty walls that crumbled like toast. My father and I worked together. He lifted up old linoleum tiles by sliding a cat-hammer underneath. My job was to carefully hammer down nails on the floorboards when he was through.

Some volunteers, like us, hoped to have a house one day.

"We're looking forward to living in a place without broken windows and leaky pipes," Mr. and Mrs. Rivera said.

My father said he couldn't wait to have a house that would have heat all winter.

My sisters were still too young to help with all the construction. But my mother told them, "Being little is no excuse not to pitch in." She had them squeeze juice from bags of lemons to make fresh lemonade. Then they took turns pouring and passing the cups all around.

At the end of the day there was always a lot of sweeping to do.

"I've never seen so much dust in my life," Mrs. Tran said, covering her nose.

My mother held a dustpan while I pushed the broom. My sisters giggled whenever they saw me wearing my safety mask.

On Saturday nights I'd be so tired, I'd practically fall asleep right after supper.

"You're doing good work," my father would say. And he'd thank me for helping our family. He'd say, "Big dreams are built little by little, and we are making a start."

In those four months I learned a lot about putting things together. Once I even found a piece of wood that my father said I could keep. I thought that maybe I could use it to make something on my own.

One day Mr. Tran gave everyone some news. The new house would be theirs!

"Everything is beautiful," Mrs. Tran said. She stood smiling inside the framed front door. She watched her daughter paint the big front room. The kitchen had shiny linoleum floors and brand-new appliances. There even was a washing machine! Upstairs was a bathroom and three carpeted bedrooms. Out back there was a place for a garden.

When the Tran family moved in, they threw a potluck supper. My father and I took care to make something extra special that night.

"Since I've been promoted to cook, I like to whip up a storm," he said.

We not only celebrated the Tran family's being the owners of their new home, but we also celebrated because we knew we were one house closer to our dream.

Things were really changing on Viola Street now. "This neighborhood looks like it's shaping up," the lady at the Soap & Go said. Volunteers were working on two more empty houses. And of course the Trans next door didn't mind when we wanted to get to work early.

This fall our family was notified that we'd be working on our own house next spring—number one-forty-six Viola Street. Whenever we pass it, my mother says, "I can imagine it finished already." I've already got my bedroom picked out. It's the one with the window by the yard.

During the winter, I made a birdhouse from my piece of wood and gave it to my mother. My mother was more than pleased about that. She said, thanks to me, now even the birds would have a nice little place to call home.

I used to dream that we had a million dollars to buy a house of our own. But in real life all it cost us was a lot of hard work. Anyway, it seems to me like all the money in the world couldn't buy us what we have now on Viola Street. It's just as my father says: Big dreams are built little by little, and we have made a start.